FAMILY ISSUES AND YOU™

YOUR FRIENDS
AND YOUR FAMILY

PETE MICHALSKI
AND VINCENT BISHOP

rosen publishing's
rosen central®

NEW YORK

For Eric Wilson and Jason Harman, two brilliant and creative individuals who left us too soon. –AW

Published in 2016 by The Rosen Publishing Group, Inc.
29 East 21st Street, New York, NY 10010

Copyright © 2016 by The Rosen Publishing Group, Inc.

First Edition

All rights reserved. No part of this book may be reproduced in any form without permission in writing from the publisher, except by a reviewer.

Library of Congress Cataloging-in-Publication Data

Michalski, Pete, author.
Your friends and your family / Pete Michalski and Vincent Bishop. – First edition.
pages cm. – (Family issues and you)
Includes bibliographical references and index.
ISBN 978-1-4994-3703-4 (library bound) – ISBN 978-1-4994-3701-0 (pbk.) – ISBN 978-1-4994-3702-7 (6-pack)
1. Parent and teenager–Juvenile literature. 2. Communication in families–Juvenile literature. 3. Teenagers–Family relationships–Juvenile literature. 4. Interpersonal relations in adolescence–Juvenile literature. 5. Friendship–Juvenile literature. I. Bishop, Vincent, author. II. Title.
HQ799.15.M53 2016
302–dc23

2015033386

Manufactured in the United States of America

CONTENTS

INTRODUCTION   4

CHAPTER ONE
YOUR PARENTS AND YOU   7

CHAPTER TWO
DEALING WITH FRIENDS   16

CHAPTER THREE
SIBLING SITUATIONS   25

CHAPTER FOUR
RULES AND RESPONSIBILITY   33

GLOSSARY   42
FOR MORE INFORMATION   43
FOR FURTHER READING   45
INDEX   46

INTRODUCTION

In your preteen and teenage years, everything seems to change so fast you can hardly keep up. Much of that change is good and necessary. Much of it can be confusing and cause problems, too.

You are gaining more independence, and your relationships are transforming as well. Your relations with family and friends when you were ten will likely have changed much by the time you turn thirteen, fifteen, and seventeen. Differences of opinion, disagreements, and the normal tensions of growing up can cause problems, including arguments. Some can even boil over into physical fights.

Your parents might not like your new best friend. Your brother or sister might get a crush on a friend of yours. Your clique might exclude another friend from hanging out, or you may be the one excluded. You might fight with your siblings

INTRODUCTION | 5

The early teens are a time of great change for everyone. Relationships with family change, and friendships with peers develop. It is a delicate terrain for anyone to negotiate.

YOUR FRIENDS AND YOUR FAMILY

over chores or personal space. The list of possible problems can seem unending. How do you manage and de-escalate problems with your friends and family?

In this book, we will look at examples of how to prevent and solve problems through effective communication. Responding to setbacks in your relationships is all part of growing up.

Family and friends matter. Knowing what to do—and what not to do—helps keeps the peace, makes things run smoothly at home, at school, and in your world in general, and usually makes relationships stronger over time. Let's take a look at how to best deal with your friends and your family.

CHAPTER ONE

YOUR PARENTS AND YOU

You may feel different around your parents lately. Feelings of frustration or impatience may seemingly have arisen out of nowhere. You may have snapped at your mother or brother at breakfast. Your father may have yelled a little loudly at hockey practice, and you suddenly wish you were a thousand miles away. Have they changed somehow? Or have you?

What's with them anyway? They never used to be so nosy, annoying, interfering, and embarrassing. You remember how much you liked spending time with them a year or two ago. Now, you almost have to push them away sometimes. It's as if they don't want to let you live your own life.

The funny thing is that while everyone has the potential to change, it is probably not your parents who have changed so dramatically. It's you.

Growing up means that your personal boundaries will shift. Privacy from parents becomes more important to young adults.

YOUR FRIENDS AND YOUR FAMILY

GROWING UP OVERNIGHT

Life may have seemed simple—that is, until you reached middle school. Before, you were a little kid, and your parents more or less ran your life. Although you might have hung out with friends from school, clubs, or in your neighborhood, you probably spent a fair amount of your free time with one or both parents. Young kids usually have a parent or older sibling around to watch over them.

When you grow, things begin to change. You are now older, probably taller and bigger, smarter, more experienced, and, hopefully, more responsible. You are probably craving more independence, both inside and outside your home. One big part of this is standing on your own two feet, without your parents always hovering. You don't love your parents any less. But you don't need or want them around so much. You also want to build your own new relationships. It is the time to build friendships of your own. As a young child, your friends may have been the children of your parents' friends. Now they are more likely to be those you meet at school or in the neighborhood.

YOUR PARENTS AND YOU | 9

> Parents might find their growing adolescents tough to deal with. This may partly be because the seemingly simpler childhood years are fresh in their minds, when their children depended on them for everything.

EXCITING (BUT COMPLICATED)

Friendships with kids your own age, who are going through the same things you are, can be one of the best things in life. Whether shooting lay-ups or darts, trading baseball cards or secrets, or even just hanging out and goofing around, there are many things that you can only do—and only want to do—with your friends.

This time in your life can be exciting. It can also be complicated. Although you might want to share some information about it with your family, you probably don't want to share everything. It is your life, and you probably want a bit of privacy. At the same time, your new independence and friendships can cause friction with your parents. They need to adjust, too, just as you do, to this new stage of your growth.

Consider your parents' perspective. Up until now, they knew most things about your life and the people in it. They are still responsible for you. Nowadays, though, you're home a lot less. You may also be confiding in friends more than in them. Parents might feel a little hurt, left out, or worried about what you are up to. Even though they're adults, parents are also humans with feelings and doubts. Consider the following scenario:

When Jenna was talking to Janice on the bedroom extension, she heard a click. Nobody was home except her mom. Could she really be listening in on her phone conversation? Janice was going on about how much she hated her father's rules. At least Janice had a father. Since Jenna's father died a year ago, it had just been her and her mom. Things had been sort of distant between them. As soon as Janice finished complaining, Jenna made an excuse and said she had to get off the phone. Then she ran downstairs.

"You were listening in on my phone conversation!" Jenna screamed.

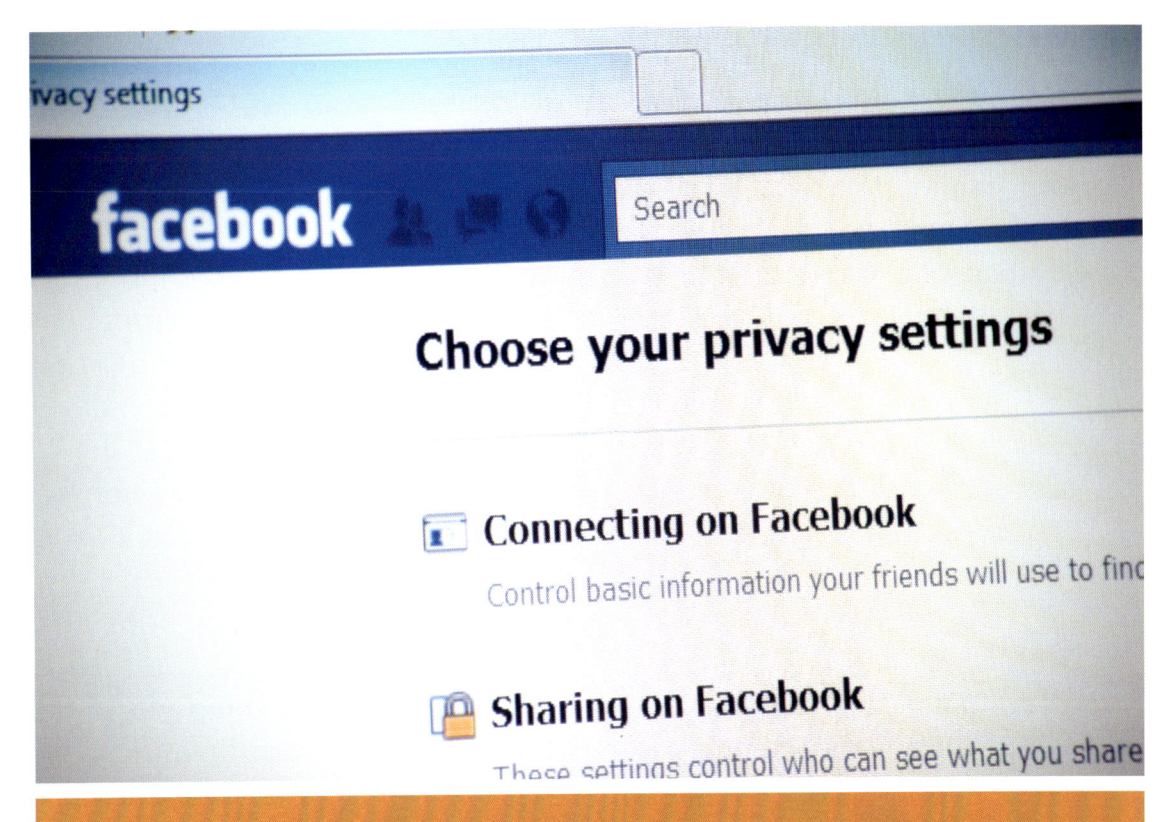

The push and pull between children and parents over privacy issues can be a tense one. Kids might want to keep things to themselves, including their social media activity, and away from the scrutiny of parents or siblings.

Her mother didn't say anything.
"Well? What's your problem?" demanded Jenna.
"Nothing," mumbled her mother.
"What do you mean 'nothing'?" Jenna was furious.
"Okay, then. The problem is you," said her mother. "Since your dad died, we never see each other. I'm at work. You're never around. But when I am home, you never talk to me anymore. It's always Janice this and Janice that. You spend more time at Janice's than here."
"So what? She's my best friend."

YOUR FRIENDS AND YOUR FAMILY

"I just want to know what's going on in your life."
"And that gives you the right to eavesdrop?"
Jenna stomped out of the house and went over to Janice's. She hated her mom and hated being at home. Not that it was much of a home anymore with her father gone and her mom always moping around. Janice's house felt more like home.

It's not unusual for communication with your parents to become more difficult. You want to spend more time on your own and with your friends. As you have more outside experiences and see what goes on in your friends' homes with their parents, you'll start to look at your home and parents with new eyes.

Up until now, your home and your family were the norm. Now you begin comparing different styles of living and different styles of parenting. Why does your mom ground you for being fifteen minutes late for dinner when Freda Walinsky's mom lets Freda eat whatever she wants, whenever she wants? Why doesn't your dad play basketball with you and your friends like Tony's dad does? Comparisons such as these might cause you to view your parents critically for the first time. The way you express such criticisms could lead to arguments.

Jenna slept over at Janice's house that night. She did no get much actual sleep, however. Jenna felt guilty about blowing up at her mother. Her mom had no right to listen in on her phone conversations or to criticize her hanging out with Janice. But it was true that Jenna rarely told her mother anything anymore. She talked much more to Janice's mom than to her own mother. And she was rarely at home. Even Janice thought that was weird. "How come we don't go to your place?" she'd ask Jenna. Jenna would make some excuse

COMMUNICATION IS KEY: FIVE TIPS

Whatever your family is like, you are going to get into arguments with a parent, both parents, or guardian. From time to time, that can even be a good thing. If something is eating away at you, it's better to get it off your chest than to stew, brood, and pretend it isn't there. The same goes for your parents. However, some ways of communicating are preferable to others.

1. Don't scream, yell, or rant. Your parents will react to your tone of voice instead of what you are actually saying.
2. Don't slam doors or stomp out of the house. It can come across as immature, and that can undermine your argument or gripe if it's a valid one.
3. Use "I" messages instead of blaming another person. For example, instead of saying, "You're always treating me like I'm a little kid!" try "I think you sometimes treat me like I'm a little kid." The first phrase puts your parent on the defensive. The second allows for discussion (and resolution) of a problem.
4. Consider your parents' feelings and point of view. In the scenarios mentioned earlier, Jenna was mad about her mother's eavesdropping, but once she looked at things from her mom's side, she realized they both had legitimate grievances.
5. Try to compromise. It helps when each side feels that the other is willing to make an effort. The fact that Jenna was going to spend more time at home with her mom and her mom supported her strong friendship with Janice is an example of compromise.

YOUR FRIENDS AND YOUR FAMILY

about her mother not liking noise in the house. But the real reason was she didn't want Janice to see her mother so depressed.

The next day after school, Jenna was nervous about going home. When she got there, her mother was sitting in the kitchen with that same sad look on her face.

Starting school or entering a new one can be difficult, especially if a student feels he or she has no friends. It is even worse if someone is targeted by bullies or excluded.

"I'm really sorry I listened in on your phone conversation," she said. "And I'm glad you have a good friend like Janice. I know she has been a big support to you. I guess I just miss your dad, and I don't want to lose you, too."

"I miss you too, Mom," said Jenna. "I really like hanging out with Janice, but I promise to stay around a bit more."

As more and more of your life takes place beyond your home, you will be exposed to new ideas and people. Other things and people, including friends, will influence your opinions and beliefs, for good or bad. Your parents might not always agree with these new ideas. They might even argue with you about them. They might consider them unproductive, negative, or even destructive. In some cases, they may even be right.

Not all new friends are a good influence. Some may be misguided or prejudiced. A new friend, for example, might look down on lesbian, gay, bisexual, transgender, and questioning (LGBTQ) people. They may casually use homophobic slurs around you. Without thinking too much about it, you may let them creep into your everyday speech. Your folks might catch you saying something inappropriate and become concerned. Do you think they might be right to criticize you?

CHAPTER TWO

DEALING WITH FRIENDS

Middle school can be a dramatically different environment than grade or elementary school. Just when you had gotten used to the same people from grade school for the past few years, you are thrust into a new environment. It might mean dealing with all kinds of new people. You may get involved in new activities, like clubs or sports. The pool of potential friends might be much bigger than before. Your relationships with old friends, whether or not they have joined you in middle school, may go through changes. You may even drift apart or lose touch entirely. Consider the following scenario:

Mark and Kerry had been best friends since kindergarten. Their mothers were best friends from high school. Because their mothers spent so much time together, Mark and Kerry did, too. They even went to the same school. Their parents were happy their children had become as close as they had been.

Mark and Kerry entered junior high, and they were both suddenly busier. Clark joined the Boy Scouts and hung out mostly with his troop and his male school friends. Kerry didn't care. She got into rock climbing and befriended some kids at school that did not know Mark.

DEALING WITH FRIENDS | 17

Athletics can be a great way to make friends in a new environment. Keeping busy and in good shape will also help take the edge off the strains of growing up and relationship tensions with friends or family.

YOUR FRIENDS AND YOUR FAMILY

One day, Kerry's mother asked her to come to a play. "You can invite Mark, too," she suggested.

"I'd rather invite Ashley," said Kerry.

"But you and Mark are such good friends. It makes me sad that you never see each other."

"Mom, you and his mom are good friends. Mark and I really don't have anything in common anymore." Telling her this seemed to make Kerry's mom a bit sad.

"I'd really like you to meet Ashley," said Kerry.

"Okay, hon," said Kerry's mother. "I'd like to meet Ashley, too."

It's nice if your parents approve of your friends. But it's probably not healthy for them to choose them for you. Nonetheless, it's important that your parents meet your friends and know who you spend time with. If your family is an important part of your life and your friends are as well, it's only normal that they at least meet each other.

Making friends can be tough. One's interests and likes (and dislikes) can change pretty often, even from one week to the next. Some kids seemingly change friends like they change their clothes. True friends, however, are those

DEALING WITH FRIENDS | 19

Finding a friend who shares your hobbies and interests is a special thing and should be cherished. Someone whose pursuits are positive and constructive might also get along with your family better, too.

who stand by you during tough times, whom you can trust, and who accept you for who you are.

Being yourself will get you the friends you deserve and wish for, even if making friends is tough at first. This can be true especially if you feel different or have felt alienated by others due to

Adolescence is likely the first time in a young person's life during which common interests and individual choice determine their peer group rather than parental choice or the neighborhood they live in.

your appearance, ethnicity, sexual orientation, religion, or other supposed difference, like being differently abled. Real friends and good people will always look past criteria that others may use to dismiss you. Another person who has felt rejected may be the first one to help you through your own experience in a new environment. Sometimes, simply being the new kid can make you a target or social pariah.

Everybody wants to belong. It can feel terrible to be on the outside. But, as many people discover, it can also hurt to be on the inside if you have to pretend to be someone that you're not. There are times when someone in middle school (and later in high school and even in college) may be tempted to pretend they like a certain type of music, or dress a certain way, or engage in other behaviors they might actually dislike or disapprove of, simply to fit in. Going against your own nature can make you feel bad. It can be as innocuous as trying to hang out with the goth or raver crowd if you don't like their music, or as extreme as standing idly by when a friend beats up someone for being different.

PEER PRESSURE, BULLYING, AND CLIQUES

Many kids hitting middle-school age feel they have to look or behave in a certain way to fit in. Some kids even insist you look or behave in a certain way or else they'll have nothing to do with you. This is called peer pressure. Even worse, those who cannot fit in, or refuse to, are persecuted in the form of bullying, whether in person or online via social media. These are problems many kids face, despite the supposed efforts of schools and other institutions that claim to fight bullying and exclusion.

When it comes to peer pressure, you might sometimes be too close to the situation to see it clearly. Sometimes your parents,

YOUR FRIENDS AND YOUR FAMILY

The need to fit in, whether it's with a group of friends or an exclusive clique, is a pressing one for young people. It is easy to feel alienated, but it is only a matter of time before you find friends of your own.

who are more experienced, might see the effects of peer pressure on you more than you do. If they criticize what they see as negative behavior or a poor choice in friends, they might have a good reason. You should at least hear them out. They only want what's best for you.

Cliques are one source of peer pressure in schools. A clique is a group of kids that hang out primarily with each other. In many cases, they actively exclude others from their group, but not always. Some cliques believe anybody that doesn't look, dress, or act like them is a geek, nerd, or loser. By definition, an exclusive clique excludes others, most of whom they look down upon. It generally wants its members to

THINKING LONG TERM: FRIENDS OR FAMILY?

Some friendships last years, while others might last a week or a month. Your family lasts forever. They are an essential part of your life, and you have to seriously question any friendship that may have a negative impact on your relationship with your parents and siblings. It is not worth it to alienate your family because you fear they will embarrass you in front of a friend. In your life, you will probably make many friends and lose a few, too. You'll only have one family.

There may arise a time when your father or mother gets angry with one or more of your friends. Maybe they come home early from a vacation and they catch your friends partying at your house. Or a friend lights a cigarette in your house, against their wishes. Your folks might interpret such an action—rightly—as rude and a bad influence on you.

The same may be true when it comes to drug use and abuse and other behavior. Even if they sometimes act strict or overprotective, your parents have every right to worry about your health and safety. In these cases, their disapproval with your life choices and choice of company is well founded.

be and act the same. Members of a clique do almost everything together.

SOCIAL MEDIA ON THE SCENE

These days, everyone seems ultra-connected through social media, cellphones, and smartphones. These can be great for catching up with friends, making plans, and just having fun. However, they can also cause and magnify problems of their own. In middle school, especially as people make new friends, become aware of sexuality, and hit other milestones, the opportunity also grows for social media to be used for exclusion, spreading rumors, and other negative activities.

Remember that anything you put online or into a text message can potentially last forever somewhere. Even the images on Snapchat can be recovered from one's phone or Snapchat's servers, even if you think they are erased. Thus, you should think twice about using social media and smartphones to harass or hurt others, gang up on them, or any other kind of harassment or exclusion.

Besides the chance you will get in trouble, you must also realize that the nature of social media means you might act impulsively. When given the chance to think about potentially hurtful actions, you might step back and realize that it's wrong to hurt people. Check yourself before you adopt a gang or wolf pack mentality. Are you really that kind of person? How would you feel if it happened to you? Because it could happen to you at any time, too. It is something to think about in a world where we are all connected, seemingly all the time, for better or worse.

CHAPTER THREE

SIBLING SITUATIONS

Most parents try to raise siblings to maintain strong relationships with each other. Brothers and sisters sometimes argue with each other, sometimes steer clear of each other, and sometimes grow up the best of friends. For many people, brothers and sisters are a big part of their lives. When someone enters middle school, his or her relationships with siblings will probably change, at least somewhat.

YOUNGER SIBLINGS

The following scenario illustrates one of many possible sibling relationships and how it changed:

Michelle, 12, and her brother Justin, 10, had always spent a lot

Having a good relationship with a sibling can go a long way in helping you feel grounded and stable. Even the occasional argument can help strengthen that bond.

of time together. Michelle was a tomboy, and she and Justin had a pack of neighborhood friends with whom they played and hung out with all the time.

Then Michelle went off to junior high, and she started hanging out with the girls in her grade. She started wearing skirts and grew her hair out.

Justin felt that Michelle wasn't interested in him anymore. She spent a lot of time at her new friend Shawna's house and almost never wanted to do anything together like they used to. He resented Shawna, especially after one run-in on the street where she whispered, "Who's the little kid?" to Michelle before they were introduced. Justin decided that if Michelle was going to ignore him, he would ignore her, too.

Michelle didn't really miss the boys from her block. They were nice enough but pretty immature. Justin was being a big pain, though. He was always sulky around her. Plus, he was pretty rude to Shawna. Deciding that he was just going through a phase, Michelle decided just to ignore Justin until he grew out of it.

When siblings relatively close in age grow up at different times, it's inevitable that at some ages they'll be much closer and have more things in common than at other ages. Even if they are close, differing personalities will yield each sibling different friends. A simple gap of two years during one's early teens can make a huge difference in how well you get along with younger or older brothers or sisters.

When older siblings enter middle school, embrace greater independence, and make new friends, for example, their younger brother or sister may feel left out. They may miss the times they used to share not so long ago. This may lead to the younger sibling resenting the older one's new friends and

LOOKING OUT FOR YOUR YOUNGER SIBLING ONLINE

Nowadays, chances are you and even your younger siblings have used social media. Officially, to prevent violation of privacy and illegal data gathering by big corporations, most social media platforms officially bar anyone younger than thirteen from joining.

Of course, many kids simply join anyway, and many use these networks responsibly. About half of ten-year-olds, by some accounts, have joined a network or used a social media app. If you have a younger sibling who is just starting to be social online and via smartphone, you might want to befriend them on one or more of these networks, with certain limits.

For example, you may limit them to certain aspects of your own online presence, since you are older and more worldly (even if you are, say, thirteen, and they are nine or ten). Your parents may also be involved, but if they do not have the time or are not tech-savvy, you may be the point person to check in on your younger brother or sister online.

Be careful to balance their need for privacy with the fact that they are your sibling and might need extra protection. Check to make sure they do not reveal too much so that others cannot exploit their online data or identities, and also that they are being good citizens on the Internet. Ask them if they are on networks like Vine, Tumblr, Instagram, or on chat/communication apps like WhatsApp or ooVoo. Don't hesitate to offer advice on how to use social media responsibly.

stirring jealousy of their new freedoms. The older sibling might be able to stay out later and stay up later at night.

It is often up to the older sibling to make a gesture of reconciliation. Naturally, you do not want a younger brother tagging along with you when you hit a movie with friends or constantly lurking around if your friends come over.

But try to see it from your sibiling's perspective and be diplomatic. You can make sure your younger brother does not feel bad. He probably looks up to you, after all. Do things with whatever spare time you have, and treat him well when the family is alone, without outside friends or visitors. This paves the way for even better sibling relations down the line. When you are twenty or thirty years old, the age differences have largely disappeared, and you can hang out and count on each other.

BEING A YOUNGER SIBLING

While younger siblings can be a source of problems at times, so can older siblings, albeit for different reasons. Consider this scenario:

The first time Eve brought her friend Hannah over to her apartment, they had a great time. At least until Hannah caught sight of Eve's sixteen-year-old brother, Miguel. "He's cute!" exclaimed Hannah, her eyes wide. Even though Miguel barely gave either of them the time of day—too busy fixing his bike out in the parking lot—Hannah was so obviously into him that Eve was embarrassed. When Hannah asked if she could grab a soda out of the fridge, Eve said of course. She didn't suspect that Hannah was going to take the soda out to Miguel and spend twenty minutes talking to him out in the parking lot. Miguel was visibly flirting back, and this just made Eve even more uncomfortable. She al-

One major bone of contention between younger and older siblings is that older ones will branch out and make friendships outside the family first. This can leave a younger sibling feeling left out.

ways liked to keep friends and family separate, especially when it came to her brother.

When Hannah finally came back inside, Eve was flustered but she played it cool. "Where did you disappear to?" she asked her friend. "Oh Eve, your brother's so great," gushed Hannah. "He's going to take me for a ride on his bike when he gets it fixed up."

"Great..." muttered Eve, and she vowed not to invite Hannah over again unless she knew Miguel would be out. A couple of days later, however, the phone rang. Eve's mother answered it and said, "It's Hannah." Eve moved to take the receiver, but her mom said: "It's not for you Eve. It's for Miguel."

When her brother got off the phone, Eve was on the offensive. "What did Hannah want?" Eve demanded sarcastically.

"She wants me to come over and watch a video."

"All alone? She didn't invite me, too?" Eve couldn't believe it.

"Nope."

"That traitor!" Eve was angry. "You're not going are you?"

"Well..." said Miguel teasingly.

"You better not. She's my friend! You better stop leading her on or..."

"Hey, cool it, Eve." Miguel interrupted her and laid a hand on his sister's shoulder. "I'm not going to go over there. I'm not interested in your prepubescent little girlfriends."

In most situations like Eve's, an older sibling probably won't be interested in a "little kid with a crush." However, he or she might be somewhat flattered by the attention. It is also obviously not a very nice situation for you to feel like an outsider around your sibling and your (supposed) best friend. If it looks as if your friend's infatuation isn't going to blow over anytime soon, it's probably a good idea to try talking to both your older sibling and your

Because you live in such close proximity, it is often a good idea not to let bad blood fester after a sibling argument. Reaching out in a spirit of compromise is probably your best bet.

friend. Miguel didn't take Hannah's crush seriously, but Eve did. When he saw how hurt and angry she was, he made it clear he wasn't interested in Hannah. Miguel's next step would be finding a way of politely making it clear to Hannah as well.

Eve could have handled herself better in the situation as well. Rather than getting upset, she could have cooled down and calmly explained to Hannah that her interest in Miguel bothered her a bit. She could also have added that being left out of Hannah's invitation also made her feel excluded.

Lastly, if Hannah was truly Eve's friend, she would consider Eve's feelings and be more thoughtful. Either she would avoid hitting on Miguel in the first place, or at least run it by Eve before flirting with him. Of course, Hannah could take her friend's feelings into consideration and still decide she wants to pursue Miguel. Eve and Hannah's situation could escalate. If Eve doesn't budge, Hannah will have to decide which means more to her: her friendship with Eve or a potential relationship with Miguel.

CHAPTER FOUR

RULES AND RESPONSIBILITY

Being older comes with more independence and agency. Many parents understand this and give their middle schoolers and teenagers more freedom than their seven- or eight-year-olds. This may mean a later curfew. For example, if you just turned eleven, you might be excited to have a 9 pm curfew during the summer, letting you hang out well into the early evening.

But with this freedom comes responsibility. Your parents will quickly rescind such privileges if you abuse them; for example, if you come home at 9:30 instead of by curfew time. Not abiding by the rules shows them you cannot be trusted. The less your parents trust you, the more worried they will be. Getting more freedom is often tied to playing by the

One of the ways some kids rebel against parental rules is by breaking them, whether blatantly or secretly, like this girl sneaking out of the house.

YOUR FRIENDS AND YOUR FAMILY

rules rather than rebelling against them. The following scenario provides an example of the negotiations that occur between kids and adults:

Even before he asked permission, Dwayne knew his mother was going to make a stink about him going to Jamal's party. He was right. Ever since his older brother, Charlie, had gotten hit by a car walking home late at night, his mom worried all the time.

"I don't want you going," she said. "I bet there'll be drugs and alcohol there, and you never know what kind of trouble you could get into."

TIME TO PARTY! (RESPONSIBLY)

One of the newest and more exciting experiences for kids hitting middle-school age is the chance to go to parties. It is up to you to assuage any fears and answer honestly any questions your parents might have about a friend hosting a party. Naturally, reassure them that the host's parents will be involved, whether they are nearby or, more likely, at home.

There are other things to remember. One, agree with your parents on a curfew time, especially if it happens to be different from your normal one due

RULES AND RESPONSIBILITY | 35

to the special occasion. Tell your parents the location of the party, who will be there, and make sure they have the information, such as phone numbers, of the parents or responsible adults involved. Make sure they know there will not be any alcohol or drug use at the party.

If you yourself are throwing a party, there are ways to do it while staying safe without having your parents become a smothering presence. Parents should be on site, but they need not linger and try to party with the guests. They need only make a couple of appearances and then retire to another part of the house, or stay outside, or wherever you have arranged with them to be.

Naturally, make sure your guests do not bring or use alcoholic beverages, drugs, or cigarettes. Plan ahead when it comes to inviting guests, making sure not to invite too many people and to ensure that no one unpredictable or unknown shows up. A whole bunch of strangers arriving at your house can be a recipe for disaster. Last but not least, make sure to set definitive start and end times for your party. Be diplomatic and polite but firm when clearing people out. Make sure to clean up properly after your guests and not to leave rudely this thankless task to other family members, especially the generous parents who let you have a party in the first place!

Dwayne was ready for this, however. He knew that if he made a big fuss and accused his mom of being unfair, she would just put her foot down even more. Instead, using a calm voice, he tried another tactic.

"Look, Mom, this party's really important to me. If it will make you feel better, you can drive me there, and we'll arrange a time beforehand for you to come pick me up. Jamal's parents are going to be home that night. If you want, I can give you their number and you can talk to them."

Although she didn't look completely satisfied by this reasoning, Dwayne's mother found her son's sensible offer pretty much impossible to refuse.

Even overprotective parents who worry too much will usually be willing to compromise if you can make them see that they have nothing to worry about. Although many parents have trouble getting used to the fact that the children they raised from babies prefer to cruise the mall with their friends than have a family board game tournament at home, many of them are simultaneously proud of their children's newfound independence.

Of course, parents will worry about you as you spend more time out of their sight and out of the house. They care about your safety. You can cut down on your parents' worries, and in doing so save yourself some headaches of your own, by being a good communicator. Always let your folks know where you are going to be, for how long, and what time you'll be home. If these plans change, call or text them and ask if it's okay to stay an hour longer at the park or to eat dinner at your friend's house. This will ease their minds and let

RULES AND RESPONSIBILITY | 37

Whenever you are out at night socializing, calling home is a good idea. This is important not simply to adhere to your parents' rules but also to avoid worrying them unnecessarily.

them know you are responsible and that you respect their concerns—and them. Sometimes, a parent's reasoning might be a bit more complicated, as in this scenario:

James had come over to Mark's place several times, and he seemed to hit it off with Mark's parents pretty well. At least that's what Mark had thought. But when he asked his parents if he could go over to James's place and spend the night, his parents exchanged funny looks and said no.

"What do you mean, no?" asked Mark. "James's parents let him come over here."

That's different, son," said Mark's dad. "This is a pretty safe neighborhood. James's neighborhood is pretty violent."

"Well, James hangs out around there."

"Mark," said his mom. "James's neighborhood is mostly black and James is black, too. You're not."

"So he can come over here to our mostly white neighborhood, but I can't go over there to his mostly black neighborhood? I think that's racist," said Mark.

"It's not because it's a mostly black neighborhood that we're concerned, Mark. It's because it's an unsafe neighborhood," said Mark's dad. "We'd be concerned about you going to a mostly white neighborhood if it was known to be unsafe."

"We like James a lot," explained Mark's mom. "But we would prefer if you had him sleep over here instead. Would that be a big problem?"

"I don't know. I'll have to think about it and then talk to James," said Mark.

You might not always agree with your parents' decisions or attitudes. Sometimes, you might even know in your gut that they are wrong. But you are their child, and they do have the right to make rules. Hopefully, these rules are based out of concern for your safety and not due to their own prejudices and stereotypes. Although Mark wasn't thrilled by his parents' argument, at least they explained their reasons and offered him another option. It then became his choice whether or not to accept that option.

Parents are human and are sometimes far from perfect. They might have ideas or opinions you really don't agree with and know are wrong. And they might not be willing to compromise. Think about how you might react to the following situation, where a parent's feelings are more straighforward and troubling:

When Jack brought Ariel over to his house for the first time, his dad acted as if Ariel didn't exist. Jack was really embarrassed by his dad's rude behavior. Ariel was the first white friend he had brought home. At his old public school, almost none of the kids had been white. Ariel was Jewish and wore a yarmulke on his head. Jack's dad was black and had converted to Islam.

After Ariel went home, Jack's dad said he wanted to talk to Jack. "I don't want that Jewish kid in my house," he announced.

"Why not?" asked Jack.

"He's white and he's . . . Jewish, and that's enough," said his dad angrily.

Jack was upset. He loved his dad. But he had never before seen what a bigot his father was. Feeling confused, he went to talk to his mom.

"Your father's a good person," said Jack's mom. "But like everybody, he has his flaws. He has some wrongheaded opinions about people that you and I don't share."

"So you're saying I can't have my friend over to my house?" demanded Jack.

40 | YOUR FRIENDS AND YOUR FAMILY

Disagreements with the older generation may center on your friendships with people from ethnicities and cultures your parents might not be familiar with. Even parents change and adapt, so be patient, and they may very well come around.

RULES AND RESPONSIBILITY | 41

"Jack, if your father doesn't want Ariel in this house, there's nothing you and I can do about it," sighed Jack's mom. "It's his house, too. And Ariel wouldn't feel good here anyway. That doesn't mean you have to stop being friends with Ariel. Your dad's your dad and you are you. You're not going to agree on everything, and that's normal. I'm sorry it makes it difficult, but I'm glad that you have a good head and can see beyond the color of someone's skin."

Dealing with difficulties with family and friends takes patience, understanding, flexibility, and a willingness to communicate. These challenges also help build these qualities within you. As you enter middle school, it helps to try to see situations from the perspectives of others. As maddening and difficult as they can be, life would not be the same without them. Doing right by them, and challenging them to do right by you, is part of growing up.

GLOSSARY

agency The ability to act, or being empowered.
bigot Someone who discriminates against others based on race, religion, or other differences.
clique A small, select group of friends.
curfew A set hour to be home.
cyberbullying A form of bullying or harassment that largely takes place online but is no less stressful or potentially crippling for its victims.
differently abled A new, less hurtful term for those who have some kind of disability, whether physical or mental.
exclusion The process or state of leaving someone out from one's group of friends or clique.
infatuation Being attracted to or having a crush on someone.
LGBTQ Stands for lesbian, gay, bisexual, transgender, or questioning and applies to anyone whose sexual orientation or identity is other than heterosexual.
norm Standard or average.
peer pressure When you feel forced into something by kids your own age.
reconciliation The act of making up after a fight or argument.
worldly Mature and experienced in life.
yarmulke A skullcap worn by religious Jewish males.

FOR MORE INFORMATION

American Association for Marriage and Family Therapy
112 South Alfred Street
Alexandria, VA 22314-3061
(703) 838-9808
Website: https://www.aamft.org/iMIS15/AAMFT
The American Association for Marriage and Family Therapy is a professional organization for therapists working to help married partners and families through difficulties related to mental and emotional disorders, addiction, health problems, and family conflict.

Big Brothers Big Sisters of America
2202 North Westshore Blvd, Suite 455
Tampa, FL 33607
(813) 720-8778
Website: http://www.bbbs.org
Big Brothers Big Sisters of America is a national organization that connects volunteers to children in need of positive older role models.

The Canadian Association for Marriage and Family Therapy (CAMFT)
P.O. Box 693
Tottenham, ON L0G 1W0
Canada
(905) 936-3338
(800) 267-2638 (Toll free)
admin@camft.ca
Website: http://camft.ca
The Canadian Association for Marriage and Family Therapy unifies professionals providing help to families and spouses in need.

Center for Parent Information and Resources
c/o Statewide Parent Advocacy Network
35 Halsey St., Fourth Floor
Newark, NJ 07102
E-mail: malizo@spannj.org
Website: http://www.parentcenterhub.org
The Center for Parent Information and Resources funds and runs resource centers for parents.

Children's Friend and Family Services
110 Boston Street, 2nd Floor
Salem, MA 01970
(978) 744-7905
Website: http://childrensfriend.net
Children's Friend and Family Services creates programs that help families with parenting issues, strained relationships, and other problems, with an emphasis on families facing economic hardship.

WEBSITES

Because of the changing number of Internet links, Rosen Publishing has developed an online list of websites related to the subject of this book. This site is updated regularly. Please use this link to access the list:

http://www.rosenlinks.com/FIY/Friend

FOR FURTHER READING

Canfield, Jack, Mark Victor Hansen, Madeline Clapps, and Valerie Howlett. *Chicken Soup for the Soul: Teens Talk Middle School: 101 Stories of Life, Love, and Learning for Younger Teens.* New York, NY: Simon & Schuster, 2011.

Espejo, Roman. *Social Networking* (Teen Rights and Freedoms) Farmington Hills, MI: Greenhaven Press, 2011.

Herron, Ron, and Val J. Peter. *A Good Friend: How to Make One, How to Be One* (Boys Town Teens and Relationships). Boys Town, NE: Boys Town Press, 2011.

Hersch, Patricia. *A Tribe Apart: A Journey into the Heart of American Adolescence.* New York: Ballantine Books, 1999.

Kamberg, Mary-Lane. *I Have Been Bullied. Now What?* (Teen Life 411). New York, NY: Rosen Publishing, 2015.

Mayrock, Aija. *The Survival Guide to Bullying: Written By a Teen.* New York, NY: Scholastic, Inc., 2015.

Morrow, Paula. *My Parents are Divorcing. Now What?* (Teen Life 411). New York, NY: Rosen Publishing, 2015.

Owens, Michael, and Amy Gelman. *I'm Depressed. Now What?* (Teen Life 411). New York, NY: Rosen Publishing, 2011.

Roberts, Emily, and Jennifer L. Hartstein. *Express Yourself: A Teen Girl's Guide to Speaking Up and Being Who You Are* (The Instant Help Solutions Series). Oakland, CA: Instant Help Books, 2015.

Van Dijk, Sheri. *Relationship Skills 101 for Teens: Your Guide to Dealing with Daily Drama, Stress, and Difficult Emotions Using DBT* (The Instant Help Solutions Series). Oakland, CA: Instant Help Books, 2015.

INDEX

A

agency, 33
alcohol, 34, 35
arguing, 4, 12, 13, 15, 25

B

brothers and sisters, 4, 11, 23, 26–28, 29
bullying, 21

C

cliques, 4, 22, 24
communication, 6, 12, 13, 36, 41
compromising, 13, 31, 36, 39
consideration, 10, 13, 15, 32
curfew, 33–34
cyberbullying, 21

D

disagreements, 4, 40
drugs, 23, 34, 35

E

exclusion, 21, 22

F

family
  communicating with, 10, 13
  problems with, 6, 41
  relationships with, 4–6, 23
fighting, 4, 21
fitting in, 21–22
friends
  making, 18, 20
  problems with, 6, 41
  relationships with, 4–6, 23
friendships, 10, 13, 23, 32

G

growing up, 4, 6, 8–9, 41

I

immaturity, 13, 26
independence, 8, 10, 26, 33, 36
infatuation, 30

L

LGBTQ issues, 15

M

making friends, 18, 20
maturing, 4, 6, 8–9, 41

P

parents, 7–15, 16, 18, 21, 23, 25, 27, 33–40
  communicating with, 12, 36
  disagreeing with, 38–39
  overprotective, 23, 36
  respecting decisions of, 38–39
partying, 34–35
peer pressure, 21–22

R

respect, 38
responsibility, 33–41
rules, 33–41

S

safety, 23, 36, 39
siblings, 4, 11, 23, 25–33
   protecting, 27
   younger, 25–32
social media, 24, 27

T

trust, 20, 33

ABOUT THE AUTHORS

Vincent Bishop has worked as a taxi driver and a painter. He is currently a writer for websites and the father of three teenagers.

Margaux Baum is an editor and writer from Queens, New York. Her books for young adults usually include books on health, hygiene, and relationships.

PHOTO CREDITS

Cover (figure) Sergey Furtaev/Shutterstock.com; cover (background), p. 1 clockwise from top left William Perugini/Shutterstock.com (top and bottom left), Monkey Business Images/Shutterstock.com, Creatista/Shutterstock.com; p. 3 sezer66/Shutterstock.com ; pp. 4-5 fstop123/E+/Getty Images; pp. 7 (top), 16, 25 (top), 33 (top) William Perugini/Shutterstock.com; p. 7 © iStockphoto.com/pierredesvarre; pp. 8-9 Betsie Van Der Meer/Taxi/Getty Images; p. 11 © iStockphoto.com/Samuel Burt; p. 14 1MoreCreative/E+/Getty Images; p. 17 strickke/E+/Getty Images; pp. 18-19 Steve Coleman/OJO Images/Getty Images; p. 20 Tony Hopewell/Digital Vision/Getty Images; p. 22 Denkou Images/Cultura/Getty Images; p. 25 Brand New Images/Iconica/Getty Images; p. 29 Yuri_Arcurs/E+/Getty Images; p. 31 JGI/Jamie Grill/Blend Images/Getty Images; p. 33 © David Young-Wolff/PhotoEdit; pp. 36-37 Yiu Yu Hoi/The Image Bank/Getty Images; pp. 40-41 © iStockphoto.com/PeopleImages; cover and interior pages patterns and textures Irina_QQQ/Shutterstock.com, ilolab/Shutterstock.com, Cluckv/Shutterstock.com, phyZick/Shutterstock.com; back cover Anna-Julia/Shutterstock.com

Designer: Michael Moy; Editor: Philip Wolny;
Photo Researcher: Nicole Baker